mel bay presents

Fiddling for Viola

traditional irish and american fiddle tunes arranged for viola

by Michael H. Hoffheimer

Cover photo: Andrea Guarneri viola, 1664
Courtesy America's Shrine to Music Museum, Vermillion, South Dakota

---

1 2 3 4 5 6 7 8 9 0

Visit us on the Web at http://www.melbay.com — E-mail us at email@melbay.com

Michael Hoffheimer

Michael Hoffheimer lives in Oxford, Mississippi and is professor of law at the University of Mississippi. Before teaching, he practiced law in Cincinnati. He has published books and articles on law, history, and philosophy. He plays fiddle with his children Joseph and Jean.

Acknowledgments

I thank William A. Bay for encouraging this project; Lisa A. Reilly, the University of Virginia, and Margaret Downie Banks, Curator at America's Shrine to Music Museum, for cheerfully responding to questions; and Christopher Noe and Linda Scott at the University of Mississippi Law Library for helping me get sources. Luanne Buchanan took the photograph on this page.

This book is dedicated to Joseph and Jean.

Table of Contents

Viola, violin, fiddle 4
Why I wrote this book 4
History of the viola 4
Tips on transition from fiddle to viola 6
Viola technique 7
Notation 7
Scales 9
Performance 11
Ornamentation 11
Sources 12

C Major Fingering

The Chanter's Tune 13
Planxty Fanny Powers 13
Obelisk 14
New Year's Song 15
Considine's Grove 15
The Glasgow Hornpipe 16
The Banks of the Suir 17
The Maid on the Green 18
St. Patrick's Day in the Morning 18
Belvidere 19
Bonaparte Crossing the Rhine 20
Belles of South Boston 21
O'Donnell's Hornpipe 22
Irish Washerwoman 23
A Fig for a Kiss 23
Lord McDonald's 24
The Eight and Forty Sisters 25
Shaw's Reel 26
The Idle Road 27
Oyster River 27
Kate Kearney 28
Flowers of Edinburgh 29
Miss McCloud's 30
The Tempest 31
Larry O'Gaff 31
Green Fields of America 32
Sault's Own Hornpipe 33
Tête-à-Tête (Head-to-Head) 34
The Best in the Bag 35
Lannigan's Ball 35
Maggie Brown's Favorite 36
Cameron's Favorite 37
Young Francis Mooney 38
The Glens of Mayo 38
Pat Touhey's Reel 39
The Lark in the Morning 39

G Major Fingering

Liverpool Hornpipe 40
The Three Sea Captains 41
The Connaughtman's Rambles 42
The Swallow Tail 42
Staten Island 43
Harvest Home 44
Sheebeg and Sheemore 45

Red Cross 46
Blind Mary 47
Off She Goes 47
Soldier's Joy 48
Hewlett 49
Lord Inchiquin 50
The Wind that Shakes the Barley 51
The Minstrel's Fancy (McElliott's Fancy) 52
Planxty Irwin 53
The Road to Lisdoonvarna 53
The Redhaired Boy 54
Irishman's Heart to the Ladies 55
Another Jig Will Do 55
Myopia 56
The Boys of Bluehill 57
The Walls of Liscarrol 58
The Battle of Aughrin 58
The Fairy Dance 59
Carolan's Concerto (Mrs. Power) 60
Hunting the Hare 61
Cincinnati Hornpipe 62
Come Dance and Sing 63
The Mullingar Races 64
Cherish the Ladies 65
Rickett's Hornpipe 66
Jimmy Holmes's Favorite 67
The Sweep's Hornpipe 68

D Major Fingering

Haste to the Wedding 69
Speed the Plow 70
Lillybullero (Protestant Boy's Jig) 71
Whiskey You're the Devil (Portsmouth Hornpipe) 72
Old as the Hills 73
Dougherty's Fancy 73
The Rose in the Garden 74
The Clock in the Steeple 75

F Major Fingering

Huntsman's Hornpipe 76
The Rock of Cashel 77
Planxty Charles Coote 78
Peerless Hornpipe 79
Carolan's Farewell to Music 80

B♭ Major Fingering

Southern Breeze (Southwind) 81
My Dermot 81
Fisher's Hornpipe 82

E♭ Major Fingering

College Hornpipe (Sailor's Hornpipe) 83
Mountain Ranger 84
The Boss 85
Vinton's Hornpipe 86
Planxty Tobias Peyton 87

Alphabetical List of Tunes 88

Viola, violin, and fiddle

The viola is like a big violin tuned four notes (one fifth) lower. It lacks the violin's high E string and adds a low C string. Because its range corresponds to that of a tenor or alto, it has sometimes been referred to in books as a tenor or alto violin.

English is the only language that has different words for violin and fiddle. Both English words probably come from the Latin word vitula. Technically, the term fiddle can mean any kind of bowed string instrument, especially the violin. Classical violinists refer affectionately to their instruments as fiddles.

However, in traditional music circles the term fiddle is reserved for folk fiddle (violin) music, and fiddling means the distinctive instrumental techniques adopted for such music. That is the way I will use the words in this book.

Why I wrote this book, who should use it, and who should not

When I searched for books for amateur fiddlers trying to make the transition to viola, the only one I found was an old collection by Whistler of classical violin music transcribed for viola. Whistler provides a solid introduction to the classical viola for the proficient violinist, but his musical selections would not appeal to most fiddlers, and he requires the player to read the alto clef.

The lack of fiddle music for viola is surprising because there has been an upsurge of interest in the viola among folk performers and amateur musicians. The viola is featured today in many different kinds of folk playing as well as in New Age and other contemporary music. Viola sales are up, and many electric fiddles and some acoustic ones are now made with five strings, which makes them viola-violins.

So I decided to put together the kind of book I myself looked for when I first took up the viola. Given the lack of fiddle music in alto notation, this book is aimed at two different groups of players—fiddlers seeking a transition to the viola, and violists seeking a collection of traditional fiddle music.

This book is not designed for beginning fiddlers or beginning violists. They should take lessons and use a good introductory violin or fiddle method book. Nor is its designed for fiddlers who want to learn classical viola technique. They, too, should take lessons and use a book like Whistler.

Tuning of viola.
Position of two lowest pegs can be reversed.

History of the viola, violin, and fiddle

The viola would probably be even more widely used today in traditional music circles if it were not considered to be somehow less authentic as a folk instrument than the violin. I want to briefly reconsider the viola's fate as a folk instrument in relation to the violin's.

The Chinese, Indians, and Arabs all had bowed string instruments, and the Arabs probably first introduced Europeans to bowed instruments. By the end of the Middle Ages a variety of bowed instruments were played in different parts of Europe, including fiedels, rebecs, liras, crwths, and viols. A painting on the ceiling of Peterborough Cathedral from about 1220 shows a musician playing a viola-sized instrument at the shoulder with overhand grip on the bow.

However, the viola and violin did not spring directly from these early bowed instruments. Instead, both the viola and violin suddenly appeared in their modern form about 1530. With their carved tops and backs, unfretted fingerboards, and overhand bow hold, they differed in sound and playability from the viols (lute-like fretted bowed instruments tuned in fourths). The only other important changes needed to perfect the violin and viola would occur in the 1800s with the adoption of longer, angled necks and the modern concave bow.

Scholars used to think the viola was older than the violin. There was some evidence for this view. The term

4

viola is older (the term violin means little viola). The earliest violins (like modern violas) lacked a high E string. And the earliest carved-top bowed instruments were viola sized. Nevertheless, most musical historians now believe the viola and violin developed at exactly the same time and were designed as different voices for ensemble performance.

In either case, the viola in its modern form is at least as old as the violin. Violas may even have been more important at first because more violas were made by the earliest makers and more were depicted in old paintings.

Soon after their invention, the violin-like instruments became the instruments of choice among professional musicians, though fretted viols remained popular with wealthy amateurs. By the 1700s the viola and violin had established their central place in classical music, which they have never lost.

Instrument from 1220*

During these same years the fiddle spread as a popular instrument, establishing its central place in instrumental folk music in a number of locations in Europe. In some areas the fiddle displaced older bowed instruments. And in some areas that lacked a tradition of bowed instruments, the fiddle also established its dominance. According to Breandan Breathnach, it is not known whether the Irish used bowed instruments before the fiddle (violin). But he cites a record from Cork that shows that soon after its introduction, children were being raised to play the fiddle.

There was much cross fertilization between classical and popular music during the 1600s and 1700s. The baroque composer Telemann praised the virtuosity of Polish fiddlers and acknowledged their influence on his music. The blind Irish harpist Turlough O'Carolan (1670-1738) admired classical composers like Corelli, and O'Carolan is said to have written *Carolan's Concerto* in response to Geminiani, an Italian classical violinist and composer.

During the formative years of modern classical and folk music, the players in both genres must often have been the same people. The techniques of classical violinists, violists, and folk fiddlers were closer than they are today. The chin rest was not invented until the 1800s, and older classical treatises illustrate grips that are much like today's fiddler's.

Classical violin tone before 1800 was closer to traditional fiddle tone. Shorter necks, unwound gut strings, and a lower standard pitch all contributed to lower string tension, yielding a softer, mellower sound. Most music was in the first position. Vibrato was avoided except for occasional ornamentation, and baroque players incorporated a variety of turns and other fingered ornaments still used by traditional fiddlers.

Fiddles, too, were tuned way below today's concert pitch, so it becomes a matter of definition whether fiddlers were playing violins tuned low or violas tuned high. Because the term fiddle can be loosely applied to either viola or violin, it is impossible to say from old accounts whether folk fiddlers employed violas as opposed to violins. Nor, it seems, can we infer from pictures or even surviving instruments that fiddlers were employing violins or violin-like tuning, for Maurice Riley claims in his *The History of the Viola* that in the 1800s even many classical viola players used small violas and violins strung as violas.

However, there is no denying that fiddlers have gravitated towards the higher pitch of the violin, and fiddle pitch has even risen during the 1900s (as has concert violin pitch). There are several reasons why fiddlers preferred the higher voice of the violin. First, the viola can be harder for amateurs to play. The physical challenges of playing larger instruments were more pronounced in the 1700s when violas were larger than today (and people were smaller.)

Andrea Guarneri viola, 1664. America's Shrine to Music Museum, Vermillion, South Dakota

Second, the greater cutting power of the violin would have made it far more appealing to folk fiddlers who needed an instrument audible in solo and small group accompaniment to dancing. It is especially doubtful that smaller violas (or violins tuned as violas) could have produced the volume required.

Third, higher violin pitch may have been more desirable because it corresponded to the range of traditional instruments like pipes and flutes that the fiddle

* The top illustration is copied from the engraving in William Sandys and Simon Andrew Forster, *The History of the Violin, and Other Instruments Played on with the Bow from the Remotest Times to the Present* (London: William Reeves, 1864), fig. 21. I have not seen any other more accurate copy. I am grateful to Prof. Lisa Reilly, an authority on architectural history, for the suggested date of the original painting (which is later than that given by Sandys and Forster).

was displacing or accompanying. Breathnach argues that Irish fiddlers' preference for higher strings shows they were mimicking the pipes (his own instrument). But because of a similar preference in other folk fiddling styles, it may have a functional explanation. The low strings, especially before they were wire-wound, may have just been too quiet.

Fourth, adequate violas with resonant lower strings were probably unavailable to folk performers. This leads us to the notorious problem with the viola—and from concerns of history to practice.

The problem with the viola

The violin is acoustically perfect—the perfect size for its pitch. Since the 1500s all violins have been made almost exactly the same size. The violin's sound box (the fiddle without the neck) is about 14 inches long.

But for a viola to be big enough to achieve acoustical perfection comparable to the violin's, the viola would have to be too large to hold in the arm. As a result, all violas represent a compromise between tone and playability. A singing lower register is particularly difficult to achieve with smaller instruments.

For this reason viola size has never been standardized. Viola makers can get different tonal benefits with different dimensions, and different players are willing to grapple with different sized instruments. Accordingly, modern violas range from $15^{1}/_{2}$ to $17^{1}/_{2}$ inches, and older ones were even larger.

Good violas are no more costly to make than good violins. But probably due to acoustic challenges, it seems harder to construct inexpensive violas with a satisfactory tone. And this, in turn, helps explain the absence of the viola in traditional fiddle music.

Traditional fiddle tone and viola tone

Fiddle tone differs from violin tone. Breathnach describes fiddle tone as sweet rather than brilliant, mellow rather than brittle. Stylistically, fiddle tone is characterized by limited changes in dynamics and lack of vibrato. Its distinctive tone is produced by a loose and high bow grip and use of the upper third of the bow (which combine to reduce the pressure of the bow on the strings); by fast bow strokes with the bow placed over the strings in a position approaching and even over the fingerboard; and, especially in older playing, by tuning below concert pitch. Many fiddlers seek out instruments that favor a darker tone color and play with bow hair flat to the string or with slack bow hair.

Such fiddling techniques tend to suppress the higher overtones, yielding a mellower tone. Some but not all of these techniques were also employed by classical violinists before 1800.

Viola tone also differs from classical violin tone. In some ways viola tone is more like traditional fiddle tone—mellower and less bright than the violin. Its sonorous melancholy voice is due only in part to the physical properties of the instrument. Like fiddle tone, distinctive viola tone is also the product of special techniques. These include full bowing with bow hair flatter to the string than for violin. Some treatises recommend drawing the viola bow with the hair perfectly flat to the string, but there is variation among players.

Viola bowing technique differs from traditional fiddle technique. The viola's acoustical properties together with its heavier bow tend to stifle sound production, requiring continual smooth (legato) bow motion to achieve the singing quality associated with the viola. Because its strings are less responsive than the fiddle's, this is not achieved easily towards the point of the bow. The lower strings are also harder to set into vibration and do not respond to light, fast fiddle bowing.

Viola fingering technique is similar to traditional fiddling technique. The lower pitch of the viola and the fact that many violists (like all fiddlers) support the instrument with their left hand also conspire to reduce the use and intensity of vibrato even by classical violists. And fiddlers who employ vibrato will need to slow it down accordingly.

Tips on transition from fiddle to viola

Even a small viola feels huge compared to a fiddle. The first challenge for the fiddler is find or adjust a viola so that it sounds good but does not cause physical distress.

shoulder and neck
The additional depth of the ribs or sides can cause discomfort for fiddlers who hold the instrument at their neck.
-Try omitting a shoulder rest if you use one for fiddling
-Try a lower chin rest
-Try the kind of chin rest that straddles the tail piece

fingers: string tension and action

The additional tension and gauge of viola strings requires additional finger pressure and can cause discomfort in fingering.

-Try synthetic gut strings or lighter gauge metal ones
-Try lowering the bridge slightly.

The bow and tone production

Viola strings are less responsive than fiddle strings and require a heavier bow. It is unlikely that most fiddle bows will be satisfactory. Viola bows have never been standardized in length. They range from the length of violin bows to an inch or so shorter. They are noticeably heavier in the hand than violin bows, though there is quite a range in weight.

Unfortunately, the slightly heavier weight of the viola bow can aggravate problems with the bow and may cause arm or fingers to become fatigued. This is not an unavoidable consequence of the weight of the bow but is due to properties of particular bows or possibly the method of holding it. Try adjusting your hold or try comparing different bows for extended periods of play.

Fiddlers will confront special challenges in sound production. First the increase in distance to the bridge requires a slight adjustment of the angles of the bow shoulder and elbow to maintain straight bowing.

-Make sure you are pulling a straight bow at a constant angle (roughly parallel) to the bridge.
-Choking up on the bow affects its weight. This can work well for the fiddle but may not pull enough sound from the viola.
-Try holding the bow at the frog like classical players.

In producing tone, it can be helpful to keep in mind the interaction of three factors described by Ivan Galamian: bow pressure, distance of bow from bridge, and speed of bow. Bow pressure can be increased by applying pressure, by playing farther from the point, and by holding the bow closer to the frog.

Tone production actually requires an adjustment of the three factors. Fiddlers recognize this when they move the bow away from the bridge during fast bowing at the point.

The following adjustments may help produce a fuller viola tone:

-In general, play closer to the bridge than on the fiddle
-As you move to lower strings, play slightly farther from the bridge with more arm weight and slower speed.
-Dig slightly into the low strings and feel the bow catch the string before playing.
-Try using the middle and lower half of bow or holding it closer to the frog.

To overcome weak tone and poor response, use more bow, and at the beginning avoid the tip of the bow.

The viola is not a violin

The viola will never attain the brightness and cutting power of the violin. Both its longer, thicker strings and its heavier bow prevent it from achieving the violin's responsiveness.

This requires the fiddler to adjust his or her playing. In general, slower response means slower fingers, slower playing, and the reduction of rolls and slides.

There is a need for constant bow motion and rapid returns in order to avoid choppy or staccato notes. And the heavier bow prevents the rapid snap-wrist bowing used in some fiddling.

For all these reasons, some fiddle pieces do not work well on the viola for most of us. On the other hand, the viola can bring new richness and depth to old fiddle favorites, and the special attributes of the viola open up a new repertoire, especially of slower airs, some of which may sound insipid on the fiddle.

Notation

The music in this book is printed on parallel staffs. The top is traditional viola notation in the alto clef. The bottom is a transposing violin notation that allows fiddlers who read the G or treble clef to play the viola by fingering it as if it were a fiddle.

On the alto clef, middle C lies on the center line, but on the transposing violin clef, middle C will be fingered and noted as a G on the D string. Thus violin fingering on the viola actually sounds or is transposed one-fifth lower than it is written.

Notation system used in this book

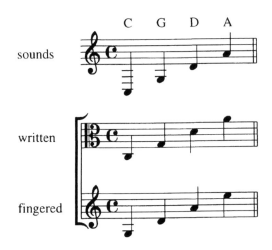

This system is easier to use than it looks. Just play one of the staff lines. Learn viola notation if you can, or play the transposing G-clef and finger the piece as if you were playing the fiddle.

Note that by transposing all notes down one fifth, we change the key itself. For example, instead of a piece starting and stopping on G, it will really start and stop on C. Music written in the key of G will actually be played in the key of C.

If you are playing with others, you can easily figure out what violin pattern fingering you should play on the viola by going up a fourth or adding a sharp (or subtracting) a flat.

> Rule: add a sharp (or subtract a flat)
> C on the viola is G fingering on the fiddle
> G is D fingering
> D is A fingering
> F is C fingering
> B♭ is F fingering
> E♭ is B♭ fingering

Although many other instruments employ transcribing notation, the transposing system used in this book will be an abomination to classical violists who pride themselves on their unique clef. (Actually, there have been many viola notation systems, and the staff positions used in this transposing system coincide with the system employed by Mersenne in the 1600s.) No doubt such a system has been proposed before, and in the early 1900s the Gibson Mandolin and Guitar Co. published music employing a common fingering system (based on the violin-mandolin's G clef) that allowed mandolin players to transfer familiar fingerings to the mandola.

C MAJOR

G MAJOR

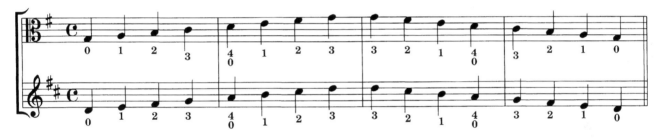

D MAJOR

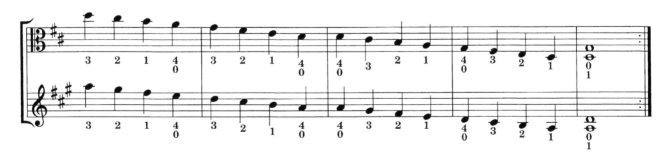

9

F MAJOR

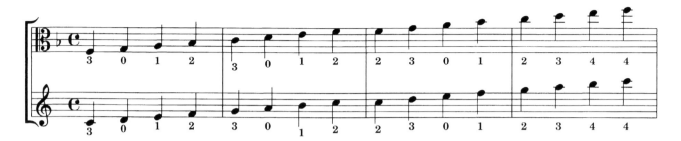

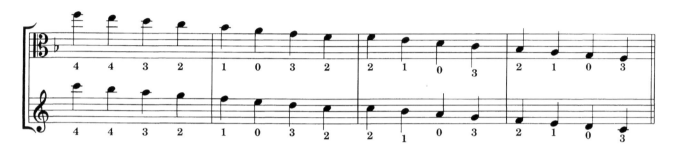

B♭ MAJOR

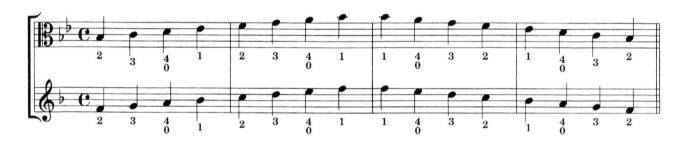

E♭ MAJOR

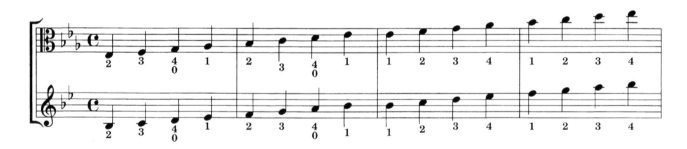

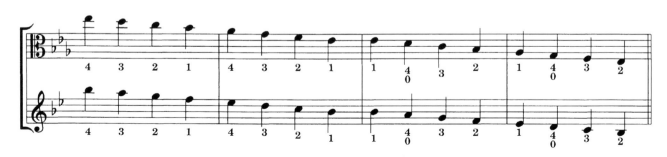

Performance

Except for set dances for groups of dancers, fiddlers often join together several dances of the same type. For example, a jig might be composed of two or more jigs, each repeated several times. The jigs thus strung together may be in different keys but would be played without interruption as a single dance. Such a dance would be followed by a contrasting dance, perhaps a group of reels played without interruption.

Fiddlers add further musical interest to simple repetitive melodies by subtly varying the melodic line, chiefly by means of ornamentation and to a lesser extent by minor variations to the melody itself. Unlike jazz improvisation, such variations almost never depart from the principal key or rhythm.

Transcriptions of fiddle music are meant merely as outlines of common versions of the principal melody. Although I have indicated a few ornaments, I have not tried to reproduce all possible drones, double stops, slides, grace notes, and other ornaments.

Common ornaments that are indicated by symbols include the shake (or trill) and the turn.

Turns

For some pieces I have given the dance type (e.g., jig, hornpipe, or reel) instead of the tempo. To be sure, there is some variation in speeds even for these dance types, and some of the reels can be played as hornpipes. They are all pretty fast. Jigs are played up tempo with a pronounced two-beats per measure: thumpity thumpity. Hornpipes are slower than reels and, even when scored entirely as eighth notes, have a pronounced two-beat swagger best indicated by a dotted eighth and sixteenth: dumdee dumdee. While reels are often played as fast as possible, they often sound better slightly slower.

I have not given full bowings, and those that I have given are meant as suggestions only. Traditional fiddlers generally observe the rule of down bow that prevailed in classical music hundreds of years ago: the down beat at the start of a measure should be played down bow. Unlike bluegrass, slurs rarely carry across bars.

Sources

Most of the tunes are taken from old collections, especially O'Neil's and Ryan's.

Barrett, Henry. *The Viola: Complete Guide for Teachers and Students.* University, Alabama:
    The University of Alabama Press, 1972.

Bodman, Lyman. *Essays on Violin Pedagogy.* Lyman W. Bodman, 1995.

Boyden, David. D. *The History of Violin Playing from its Origins to 1761 and its Relationship
    to the Violin and Violin Music.* London: Oxford University Press, 1965.

Breathnach, Breandan. *Folk Music and Dances of Ireland.* Dublin: The Talbot Press, 1971.

Bunting, Edward. *The Ancient Music of Ireland.* Dublin: Hodges and Smith, 1840.

Darley, Arthur Warren and McCall, Patrick Joseph, *The Darley & McCall Collection of Traditional Irish Music.*
    Cork: Ossian Publications, 1984 (originally published 1914).

Ivan Galamian. *Principles of Violin Playing & Teaching.* 2d. ed. Englewood Cliffs,
    New Jersey: Prentice-Hall, Inc., 1985.

The New Grove Violin Family. W.W. Norton & Co., 1989.

Nelson, Sheila M. *The Violin and Viola.* New York: W.W. Norton & Company, 1972.

O'Carolan, Turlough. *The Complete Works of O'Carolan.* Ossian Publications, 1984.

O'Neil, Francis. *O'Neil's Music of Ireland.* Mel Bay, n.d. (originally published 1907).

O'Neil's Music of Ireland. Revised by Miles Krassen. New York: Oak Publications, 1976.

Ryan, William Bradbury. *Ryan's Mammoth Collection of Fiddle Tunes.* Edited by Sky, Patrick.
    Pacific, Missouri: Mel Bay, 1995 (originally published 1833).

Riley, Maurice W. *The History of the Viola.* Ann Arbor: Braun-Brumfield, 1980.

Sandys, William and Forster, Simon Andrew. *The History of the Violin, and Other Instruments
    Played on with the Bow from the Remotest Times to the Present.* London: William Reeves, 1864.

Sitt, Hans. *Practical Viola Method.* Rev. ed. by W.F. Ambrosio. New York: Carl Fischer, Inc., 1924.

Whistler, Harvey S. *From Violin to Viola: A Transitional Method.* Milwaukee: Rubank, Inc., 1947.

THE CHANTER'S TUNE

PLANXTY FANNY POWERS

Turlough O'Carolan

A planxty is a piece of music dedicated to someone, not a kind of music. This piece may have begun as a jig, but it is now played more slowly.

OBELISK

NEW YEAR'S SONG

CONSIDINE'S GROVE

The open g's (d's) can also be played sharp.

THE GLASGOW HORNPIPE

THE BANKS OF THE SUIR

THE MAID ON THE GREEN

ST. PATRICK'S DAY IN THE MORNING

18

BELVIDERE

BONAPARTE CROSSING THE RHINE

March

BELLES OF SOUTH BOSTON

O'DONNELL'S HORNPIPE

IRISH WASHERWOMAN

A FIG FOR A KISS

23

LORD McDONALD'S

THE EIGHT AND FORTY SISTERS

SHAW'S REEL

THE IDLE ROAD

OYSTER RIVER

KATE KEARNEY

FLOWERS OF EDINBURGH

MISS McCLOUD'S

THE TEMPEST

LARRY O'GAFF

GREEN FIELDS OF AMERICA

SAULT'S OWN HORNPIPE

TÊTE – À – TÊTE
(Head – to – Head)

THE BEST IN THE BAG

LANNIGAN'S BALL

MAGGIE BROWN'S FAVORITE

CAMERON'S FAVORITE

YOUNG FRANCIS MOONEY

THE GLENS OF MAYO

PAT TOUHEY'S REEL

THE LARK IN THE MORNING

Also known as "The Trip to Sligo." This setting is taken from O'Neill who scored the open g (d) notes in part A as a (e) flats, but it is usually played this way.

LIVERPOOL HORNPIPE

THE THREE SEA CAPTAINS

THE CONNAUGHTMAN'S RAMBLES

THE SWALLOW TAIL

STATEN ISLAND

HARVEST HOME

SHEEBEG AND SHEEMORE

Turlough O'Carolan

RED CROSS

BLIND MARY

Turlough O'Carolan

OFF SHE GOES

47

SOLDIER'S JOY

HEWLETT

Turlough O'Carolan

LORD INCHIQUIN

Turlough O'Carolan

THE WIND THAT SHAKES THE BARLEY

THE MINSTREL'S FANCY

(McElliott's Fancy)

PLANXTY IRWIN

Turlough O'Carolan

THE ROAD TO LISDOONVARNA

Jig

THE REDHAIRED BOY

IRISHMAN'S HEART TO THE LADIES

ANOTHER JIG WILL DO

MYOPIA

THE BOYS OF BLUEHILL

The grace note cuts can also be played with the third finger as g's (d's).

THE WALLS OF LISCARROL

THE BATTLE OF AUGHRIN

THE FAIRY DANCE

CAROLAN'S CONCERTO

(Mrs. Power)

Turlough O'Carolan

Allegro

HUNTING THE HARE

CINCINNATI HORNPIPE

COME DANCE AND SING

THE MULLINGAR RACES

CHERISH THE LADIES

RICKETT'S HORNPIPE

JIMMY HOLMES'S FAVORITE

The dit-dah (sixteenth - dotted eighth) rhythm pattern is common in Scots fiddle music.

THE SWEEP'S HORNPIPE

This is called "Great Western" in Ryan's collection and "Great Eastern" in O'Neill's table of contents.
It is also known as "Lancashire."

HASTE TO THE WEDDING

SPEED THE PLOW

LILLYBULLERO

(Protestant Boys' Jig)

WHISKEY YOU'RE THE DEVIL

(Portsmouth Hornpipe)

OLD AS THE HILLS

DOUGHERTY'S FANCY

THE ROSE IN THE GARDEN

THE CLOCK IN THE STEEPLE

O'Neil's collection included this and an almost identical reel called "The Linen Cap."

HUNTSMAN'S HORNPIPE

THE ROCK OF CASHEL

PLANXTY CHARLES COOTE

Turlough O'Carolan

PEERLESS HORNPIPE

CAROLAN'S FAREWELL TO MUSIC

Turlough O'Carolan

SOUTHERN BREEZE
(Southwind)

MY DERMOT

Attributed to O'Carolan in O'Neil's collection.

FISHER'S HORNPIPE

COLLEGE HORNPIPE

(Sailor's Hornpipe)

MOUNTAIN RANGER

THE BOSS

VINTON'S HORNPIPE

PLANXTY TOBIAS PEYTON

Turlough O'Carolan

Alphabetical List of Tunes

Another Jig Will Do	55
The Banks of the Suir	17
The Battle of Aughrin	58
Belles of South Boston	21
Belvidere	19
The Best in the Bag	35
Blind Mary	47
Bonaparte Crossing the Rhine	20
The Boss	85
The Boys of Bluehill	57
Cameron's Favorite	37
Carolan's Concerto (Mrs. Power)	60
Carolan's Farewell to Music	80
The Chanter's Tune	13
Cherish the Ladies	65
Cincinnati Hornpipe	62
The Clock in the Steeple	75
College Hornpipe (Sailor's Hornpipe)	83
Come Dance and Sing	63
The Connaughtman's Rambles	42
Considine's Grove	15
Dougherty's Fancy	73
The Eight and Forty Sisters	25
The Fairy Dance	59
A Fig for a Kiss	23
Fisher's Hornpipe	82
Flowers of Edinburgh	29
The Glasgow Hornpipe	16
The Glens of Mayo	38
Green Fields of America	32
Harvest Home	44
Haste to the Wedding	69
Hewlett	49
Hunting the Hare	61
Huntsman's Hornpipe	76
The Idle Road	27
Irishman's Heart to the Ladies	55
Irish Washerwoman	23
Jimmy Holmes's Favorite	67
Kate Kearney	28
Lannigan's Ball	35
Larry O'Gaff	31
The Lark in the Morning	39
Lillybullero (Protestant Boys' Jig)	71
Liverpool Hornpipe	40
Lord Inchiquin	50
Lord McDonald's	24
Maggie Brown's Favorite	36
The Maid on the Green	18
The Minstrel's Fancy (McElliott's Fancy)	52
Miss McCloud's	30
Mountain Ranger	84
The Mullingar Races	64
My Dermot	81
Myopia	56
New Year's Song	15
Obelisk	14
O'Donnell's Hornpipe	22
Off She Goes	47
Old as the Hills	73
Oyster River	27
Pat Touhey's Reel	39
Peerless Hornpipe	79
Planxty Charles Coote	78
Planxty Fanny Powers	13
Planxty Irwin	53
Planxty Tobias Peyton	87
Red Cross	46
The Redhaired Boy	54
Rickett's Hornpipe	66
The Road to Lisdoonvarna	53
The Rock of Cashel	77
The Rose in the Garden	74
St. Patrick's Day in the Morning	18
Sault's Own Hornpipe	33
Shaw's Reel	26
Sheebeg and Sheemore	45
Soldier's Joy	48
Southern Breeze (Southwind)	81
Speed the Plow	70
Staten Island	43
The Swallow Tail	42
The Sweep's Hornpipe	68
The Tempest	31
Tête-à-Tête (Head-to-Head)	34
The Three Sea Captains	41
Vinton's Hornpipe	86
The Walls of Liscarrol	58
Whiskey You're the Devil (Portsmouth Hornpipe)	72
The Wind that Shakes the Barley	51
Young Francis Mooney	38

Made in the USA
San Bernardino, CA
26 January 2016